A SLEEP-OVER VISIT

By Jack Dale

Illustrated by Tom Tierney

A GOLDEN BOOK • NEW YORK

Western Publishing Company, Inc., Racine, Wisconsin 53404

Today was the big day. Michael finished his lunch and
jumped up from the table.

"Don't forget to clear the dishes before you pack,"
Michael's mother said.

Michael was going to spend the night with his friend
Jim at Jim's house. It would be the very first time
Michael had ever slept away from home. But first he
had to do his chores.

Michael cleared the dishes from the table. He cleaned the table with a sponge.

"Thank you, sweetheart," said his mother.

Michael went to his bedroom to pack his clothes. He put pajamas, socks, underwear, and a clean shirt in his backpack. Then he added his flashlight, his racing cars, and his toothbrush and toothpaste.

Red, Michael's dog, followed him when he brought his backpack downstairs. Michael hugged Red. Red's shiny fur felt silky.

"I'll be back soon," Michael said. Red whined and went to the door.

Mom held Red while Dad and Michael slipped outside. Michael felt bad. Red really wanted to come with him. But Michael knew he had to leave him behind.

Dad walked Michael to Jim's house. It was at the end of the block.

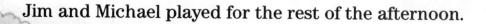

Jim and Michael played for the rest of the afternoon.

They played catch.

They raced their racing cars
on Jim's track.

They played a
video game.

At dinner, Michael ate things he had never eaten before. One thing looked like a pine cone. It was called an artichoke. Jim showed Michael how to pull off the leaves and dip them in butter.

When the boys were in their pajamas, Jim's mother and father thought of a special treat. They let Jim and Michael pop some popcorn. The popcorn pushed up the foil top of the container like a silver balloon.

Soon it was time for bed. Michael and Jim bounced on their beds. They laughed and laughed.

"Quiet down, boys!" Jim's mother called from the doorway. "Go right to sleep, now. No more playing."

Jim and Michael dove under the covers and tried to stop their giggles. Jim's mom put out the light. She left the door open a crack.

"Are you awake?" whispered Jim in the darkness.
"Yes. Are you?" Michael whispered back.
Michael and Jim whispered for a long time. This was one of the best parts of spending the night.
Finally Jim turned over and went to sleep.

Michael's eyes were wide open. He missed his mom and dad and Red. "I wish Red were here," he thought.

But then Michael thought about all the fun he was having at Jim's house. He felt very grown-up spending the night away from home. He snuggled down into the covers and fell asleep.

Suddenly Michael sat up. His blankets had
fallen on the floor, and he was cold. It was the middle
of the night. Michael heard noises downstairs. He heard
whining and scratching. He got out of bed.

"Hey, Jim, listen to that," Michael said, shaking Jim's
shoulder. "I think I hear Red."

Jim got up, too. Michael turned on his flashlight, and
the boys went downstairs.

The scratching was coming from the back door. Jim turned the latch and opened the door. Red rushed in.

"Red! Why aren't you at home?" Michael asked. Red jumped up and put his paws on Michael's shoulders. Then he jumped down and danced around the kitchen.

"Shh. Come with us," said Michael. He and Red and Jim climbed the stairs.

"Red must have missed me," said Michael when they got back to Jim's room. "He sleeps in my room at home. Let's make a bed for him between our beds."

"Okay," said Jim.

They pulled the pillows and the rest of the blankets down on the floor, and curled up with Red.

The next morning there was a knock at the bedroom door. "Your dad is on the phone, Michael," called Jim's mom.

Michael and Red got out of their warm nest and went downstairs to the phone.

"Hello, Michael," said Dad. "Have you seen Red? He must have gotten out last night."

Red stuck his face up to Michael's and licked him. "Stop it, Red! That tickles!" said Michael. "He's here with me, Dad. Don't worry. We'll see you soon."

After breakfast Michael got ready to walk home.

"Thank you for letting me sleep over," he said to Jim's mom and dad.

"Come back soon," Jim's mom said.

"I sure will," said Michael. He patted Red. "But next time *you* stay home! Now I know I can visit overnight all by myself."